I0797546

BEST FEMALE GYMNASTS
OF ALL TIME

BY ERIN NICKS

An Imprint of Abdo Publishing
abdobooks.com

abdobooks.com

Published by Abdo Publishing, a division of ABDO, PO Box 398166, Minneapolis, Minnesota 55439.

Printed in the United States of America, North Mankato, Minnesota
042020
092020

Cover Photo: Kunihiko Miura/The Yomiuri Shimbun/AP Images
Interior Photos: Kunihiko Miura/The Yomiuri Shimbun/AP Images, 5; Laurence Griffiths/Getty Images Sport/Getty Images, 6–7; Leonard Zhukovsky/Shutterstock Images, 9; Keystone Press/Alamy, 11; Ms/AP/Shutterstock/Rex Features, 13; The Asahi Shimbun/Getty Images, 14; The Picture Art Collection/Alamy, 16; AP Images, 19, 21; Sadayuki Mikami/AP Images, 22; John Gaps III/AP Images, 25; Paul Kitagaki Jr./Sacramento Bee/Tribune News Service/Getty Images, 26; Dimitri Iundt/Corbis/VCG/Corbis Sport/Getty Images, 28

Editor: Charly Haley
Series Designer: Megan Ellis

Library of Congress Control Number: 2019954367

Publisher's Cataloging-in-Publication Data

Names: Nicks, Erin, author.
Title: Best female gymnasts of All Time / by Erin Nicks
Description: Minneapolis, Minnesota : Abdo Publishing, 2021 | Series: Gymnastics zone | Includes online resources and index.
Identifiers: ISBN 9781532192340 (lib. bdg.) | ISBN 9781098210243 (ebook)
Subjects: LCSH: Gymnastics--Juvenile literature. | Gymnastics for women--Juvenile literature. | Sports--History--Juvenile literature. | Gymnastics for children--Juvenile literature.
Classification: DDC 796.44--dc23

CONTENTS

CHAPTER 1

SIMONE BILES MAKES HISTORY

When Simone Biles stepped onto the competition floor, all eyes were on her. It was October 2019. Biles was competing at the World Championships in Stuttgart, Germany. She had already performed well during the meet. In the team competition earlier in the week, she had put up huge marks on the vault and floor exercises. These high scores helped the United States win the team gold for the fifth straight year.

Simone Biles performs on balance beam at the World Championships in 2019.

LONGINES

On the last day of the meet, Biles was competing in the individual balance beam event. After she finished her routine, she sat down in the seat reserved for the last competitor. Sitting next to Biles was Liu Tingting of China, who was leading the event. Biles waited to see her own score. She could make history. When the scoreboard finally flashed her total, Biles jumped out of her seat and danced with joy. Her mark of 15.066 gave her the gold. With this medal, Biles became the gymnast with the most wins in World Championships history. Clinching the gold on the beam gave her 24 medals at

Biles uses difficult skills in her competitions. Some of her moves are named after her.

the World Championships. Eighteen of those were gold.

BILES HAS THE MOVES

Biles has reached rock-star status in the world of gymnastics. She has four moves named after her—one on beam, one on vault, and two in the floor exercise. She introduced the "Biles II" move during the 2019 World Championships. She performed it during her floor routine. It featured two backflips and three twists.

At the same event, she used the "Biles" beam dismount. It involves a double-twisting double tuck. These moves are difficult. When she lands them, Biles scores very high marks.

Biles has also won on the biggest sports stage in the world, the Olympics. At the 2016 Olympics in Rio de Janeiro, Brazil, Biles won five medals for Team USA. She helped her squad win the team gold. She also won gold in the individual all-around event, vault, and floor exercise. Her fifth medal came on beam, where she

WHAT'S IN A NAME?

It's not easy for gymnasts to have a trick or dismount named after them. They must be the first to perform and land it successfully at a World Championships, a Youth Olympic Games, or an Olympic Games. Other gymnasts with moves named after them include Olga Korbut, Victoria Moors, Cheng Fei, and Betty Okino.

Biles, *right*, celebrates with the Team USA gymnastics group known as the Final Five at the 2016 Olympics.

clinched bronze. Biles and American swimmer Katie Ledecky tied for the most medals won by women at the 2016 Olympics. With her precise routines, incredible strength, and bright smile, Biles has become one of the most memorable and successful gymnasts in history.

CHAPTER 2

PIONEERS OF THE GYM

In the early days of the Olympics, female gymnasts were only allowed to participate in team competitions. One event from 1928 looked like an early version of the floor exercise. In 1952 women began competing in separate events.

One of the greatest women to compete back then was Agnes Keleti of Hungary. Keleti had a talent for gymnastics. But she had to go into hiding during World War II (1939–1945) because her family was Jewish. The Nazi Party of Germany

Hungarian gymnast Agnes Keleti performs a routine in 1957.

killed many Jewish people during the war. But Keleti survived.

Keleti was 31 when she competed in her first Olympics in Helsinki, Finland. It was 1952. Most of the women Keleti competed against were much younger than her. She won gold for her floor exercise and bronze on the uneven bars. She also won silver and bronze for team competitions. She added to that total at the 1956 Summer Olympics in Melbourne, Australia. She won gold again for her floor exercise. She also won gold on the uneven bars and balance beam. Her Hungarian squad won gold and silver in separate team events, and Keleti also clinched a silver in the all-around competition.

VERA ČÁSLAVSKÁ

Vera Čáslavská is the only gymnast in history to win Olympic gold in every individual event for women: all-around, floor exercise, balance beam, vault, and uneven bars. She won these medals

Vera Čáslavská delivers a gold-winning performance on bars in the 1964 Tokyo Olympics.

throughout the course of her Olympic career. Čáslavská won a total of seven gold medals and four silvers in three Olympic Games (1960, 1964, and 1968).

Čáslavská competed for Czechoslovakia. She spoke out against the Soviet Union's invasion of her country before the beginning of the 1968 Olympics in Mexico. Because of this,

Larissa Latynina finished her Olympic career in 1964, after winning 18 medals across various gymnastics events.

Czechoslovakia's government wanted to arrest her. She ran away to the mountains. She trained for gymnastics by swinging on trees. She practiced her floor routine in a meadow. The Czech government eventually gave Čáslavská permission to travel to Mexico for the Olympics. She ruled the competition, scooping up four golds for floor exercise, uneven bars, vault, and the all-around event. She also won silvers on the balance beam and for team competition.

SUCCESSFUL SOVIETS

The Soviet Union sent many talented gymnasts to the Olympics during the 1950s and 1960s. Larissa Latynina was one of the most successful during this time. She was known for the graceful movements in her routines. Throughout her career, Latynina won nine Olympic gold medals—the most of any gymnast. She is also one of only three women to win the same event three times in a row. She won three straight Olympic golds in floor exercise in 1956, 1960, and 1964.

Polina Astakhova competes at the 1960 Olympics in Rome, Italy.

During those three Olympics, she won a total of 18 medals. This was an all-time record number of medals for any Olympian until 2012, when American swimmer Michael Phelps broke Latynina's record.

Polina Astakhova was another great Soviet athlete. As a child, Astakhova was very sick with tuberculosis, a lung disease. But she recovered and became a gymnast. She competed in the Olympics in 1956, 1960, and 1964. In that time, she won five gold, two silver, and three bronze medals, including back-to-back golds on the uneven bars.

CHAPTER 3

SUPERSTARS OF THE 1970s AND 1980s

The sport of gymnastics exploded in popularity around the world, thanks to superstar women in the 1970s and 1980s. They included Olga Korbut of the Soviet Union and Nadia Comăneci of Romania. Jaws dropped when Korbut performed a backflip during her routine on the uneven bars at the 1972 Olympics in Munich, West Germany. The move became known as the "Korbut Flip." Korbut won four

Olga Korbut does a backflip on the balance beam. She is known for her daring moves.

gold medals and two silvers during the 1972 and 1976 Olympics.

Comăneci became famous around the world after she scored seven perfect 10s at the 1976 Olympics in Montreal, Canada. Comăneci won a total of five gold, three silver, and one bronze medal at the 1976 and 1980 Olympics.

Lyudmila Turishcheva was another star from the Soviet Union. She won over the judges with her elegance and graceful style. During the 1968, 1972, and 1976 Olympics, she won a total of four gold, three silver, and two bronze medals.

MORE PERFECT 10s

At the 1984 Olympics in Los Angeles, California, American gymnast Mary Lou Retton charmed both the judges and the hometown crowd. She scored perfect 10s on balance beam and floor exercise. Retton won five medals at the 1984 Olympics, including a gold in the all-around event. Fans loved Retton's

Mary Lou Retton quickly became a crowd favorite after her dominating performance in the 1984 Los Angeles Olympics.

bubbly personality. Her picture was everywhere, from magazines to cereal boxes.

In 1988 Daniela Silivaş of Romania matched Comăneci's seven perfect 10s at the 1988 Olympics in Seoul, South Korea. She was a sharp performer. Silivaş missed the all-around gold by just 0.025 points to Yelena Shushunova of

Daniela Silivaş competes on balance beam during the all-around competition in the 1988 Olympics in Seoul.

the Soviet Union that year. But she still managed to win gold in floor exercise, uneven bars, and balance beam. She also won silvers in the all-around and team events, and bronze in vault.

COMPETING AFTER SURGERY

Six weeks before the 1984 Olympics, Mary Lou Retton injured her knee and needed surgery. Fans only found out about the operation after her amazing performance at the Olympics.

CHAPTER 4

MODERN STARS

The sport of gymnastics kept growing in the 1990s. The United States sent many amazing gymnasts to the Olympics. Shannon Miller was one athlete who stood out. Miller's graceful style made her one of the most successful gymnasts in US history.

She scooped up two silver and three bronze medals at the 1992 Olympics in Barcelona, Spain. Miller missed the gold medal in the individual all-around event by .012 points. Tatiana Gutsu of the Unified Team clinched the gold. Miller was viewed as the leader of the American

Shannon Miller helped lead Team USA to gold in the 1996 Olympics in Atlanta, Georgia.

Atlanta 1996

squad known as the "Magnificent Seven." Her teammates were Dominique Moceanu, Dominique Dawes, Kerri Strug, Amy Chow, Amanda Borden, and Jaycie Phelps. Miller went on to win gold on the beam as well as a team gold in Atlanta, Georgia, in 1996.

TOUGH TEAMMATES

In 2008 the American team was loaded with talent yet again. At the Olympics in Beijing, China, that year,

Nastia Liukin won a silver medal for her balance beam performance at the 2008 Beijing Olympics.

Nastia Liukin clinched five medals, including a gold in the all-around event. Liukin had the delicate moves of a ballet dancer combined with awesome athletic strength. Liukin had to battle against her friend and teammate Shawn Johnson in many of the events. Johnson ended up winning four medals during the Olympics. She finished second behind Liukin in the all-around, earning the silver medal. However, she captured her own gold medal on the balance beam.

The brilliant Simone Biles came onto the scene in 2016 and has also performed alongside some amazing American talent. One of Biles' strongest Olympic teammates was Aly Raisman. At the 2012 and 2016 Olympics, Raisman captured a total of six medals, including three golds, two silvers, and one bronze.

RUSSIA OWNS THE UNEVEN BARS

When she was a child, Russian Svetlana Khorkina was told she was too tall to be a gymnast.

Svetlana Khorkina competes on the uneven bars. She was able to use her height as an advantage in this event.

But that changed after she met coach Boris Vasilevich Pilkin. He knew her height of 5 feet, 4 inches (1.6 m) could help her in certain events including the uneven bars. This event made Khorkina famous. She earned the nickname "Queen of the Uneven Bars" by winning back-to-back Olympic gold medals in 1996 and 2000. She won a total of seven Olympic medals between 1996 and 2004.

Another Russian gymnast who dominated the uneven bars was Aliya Mustafina. She performed brilliantly on the apparatus during the 2012 and 2016 Olympics, winning back-to-back gold medals. She also clinched two team silver medals, two bronze medals in the individual all-around event, and a bronze in floor exercise.

As the sport of gymnastics continues to gain popularity, young girls in many countries will be practicing their best moves in gyms and arenas around the world. Each year more women will join the growing list of the greatest gymnasts in history.

GLOSSARY

ALL-AROUND

When gymnasts compete in all of the events as an individual. The all-around champion earns the most points from all the events combined.

APPARATUS

Equipment used for gymnastics.

CLINCHED

Confirmed or finalized, such as one's finish in a competition.

DISMOUNT

To land after performing on the vault, pommel horse, balance beam, horizontal bar, uneven bars, rings, or parallel bars.

FLOOR EXERCISE

An event in which gymnasts perform tumbling skills and dance elements on a spring-filled square mat.

PRECISE

Exactly right.

TEAM EVENT

A gymnastics event in which all members of a team compete together.

UNEVEN BARS

An event in which female gymnasts swing between two bars of unequal height.

VAULT

An event in which gymnasts push off a table and do flips and twists in the air.

MORE INFORMATION

BOOKS

Lawrence, Blythe. *Best Male Gymnasts of All Time.* Minneapolis, MN: Abdo Publishing, 2020.

McAneney, Caitie. *Simone Biles: Greatest Gymnast of All Time.* New York: Powerkids Press, 2018.

Scheff, Matt. *Aly Raisman.* Minneapolis, MN: Abdo Publishing, 2017.

ONLINE RESOURCES

To learn more about the best female gymnasts of all time, please visit abdobooklinks.com or scan this QR code. These links are routinely monitored and updated to provide the most current information available.

INDEX

ABOUT THE AUTHOR

Erin Nicks is from Thunder Bay, Ontario, Canada. She has written about sports for various websites and newspapers for over 20 years. She currently resides in Ottawa, Ontario, Canada.